MW00973150

Farleigh village was composed of a few houses.—*Page 1.*

WANDERING MAY

~ or ~

"Come Unto Me"

By

Mary L. Code

Grace & Truth Books
Sand Springs, Oklahoma

ISBN # 1-58339-114-2
Originally published by Kilmarnock; John Ritchie
Current printing, Grace & Truth Books, 2003

All rights reserved, with the exception of brief quotations.
For consent to reproduce these materials, please contact the
publisher

Cover design by Ben Gundersen

Grace & Truth Books
3406 Summit Boulevard
Sand Springs, Oklahoma   74063
Phone: 918 245 1500

www.graceandtruthbooks.com
email: gtbooksorders@cs.com

TABLE OF CONTENTS

"Supper's ready, Father," she said cheerfully, as he came
near.—*Page 7.*

WANDERING MAY

CHAPTER 1

FARLEIGH VILLAGE

A very lovely place outwardly was May Wood's village home; far away from any city, amongst the trees, and hills, and fields, where no business drew people from the nearest town, it nestled quietly and peacefully in the shadow of a grassy hill, which the country people had named the Half-way, because it rose at an equal distance between the two nearest hamlets.

Farleigh itself was but a very small village; it was only composed of a few houses, occupied by some of the labourers on the farms which lay around.

But although the green hills, fields, and trees, where the sun shone brightly, and the little river sparkled and smiled, seemed joying in their summer light, and the little thatch-covered cottages looked as if the people who lived there might be very peaceful and happy, Farleigh was not a happy place; for the summer sun looked down on a great deal of wretchedness and sin; and when the moon shed her soft light on a peaceful scene of beauty, she might have told stories of sadness and sorrow of which no one would have dreamed.

Farleigh could not be happy, because the blessed God was not known there; and perhaps there was not one in all the hamlet who loved the Lord Jesus Christ. Some of the people, no doubt, had heard the gospel message; but their hearts had not answered to it. For the most part the people lived on, and toiled on, in a sad state of ignorance; and amongst the children who were growing up untaught and uncared for, perhaps none were more so than May Wood, when she had reached the age of twelve years.

May's home was a rough thatched cottage, standing just outside the rest of the houses. If you had seen it, very likely you would have said that it was so pretty as to deserve a great deal of attention and care; for the roses and sweet jessamine that clustered round the doorway needed a careful hand to train them; and there seemed to be more to be done in the house and garden work together than a twelve-years-old pair of hands could well manage, even although they belonged to such a hard-working little maiden as May Wood.

For she was mistress of the cottage. A year ago her mother had died, after a lingering illness, when her strength had gradually weakened; and the housework had become May's charge. And then her mother had closed her eyes forever, and she had followed the black-covered coffin, holding her father's hand, to the cemetery, which lay three miles from their cottage.

The neighbours had said that "that bit of a girl" would never be able to get on by herself; but May was a brave little soul, and she determined that she would try. Trying is the best way of succeeding; and as Thomas Wood was not very particular, so long as there was a hot supper awaiting him when he came home from his day's work, and a good fire to welcome him in the winter evenings, he was contented to let things go on as they were.

Thomas Wood was not an unkind father; on the contrary, he was fond of his "little maid," as he called her; and he liked, when his work was over, and he sat on the summer evenings just within the rose-covered door, to have her near him, and to hear her talk about the neighbours' doings and sayings; or to listen to her singing some of the songs that her mother had sung to her from the time when she was a little toddling baby.

Only of late these quiet summer evenings, when May and her father had sat at the door together, had become few and far between. He did not come home so regularly as he had done before, and on the evenings when he came he would go out again when he had finished his supper, telling May that she need not sit up for him, because he would be in by and by. And when the weekly purchases had to be made, and they went together to the next village, her father seemed almost to grudge the money they spent on the things that must be had, and May had heard him several times lately asking the man at the shop to trust him for some of the money for a little time. She could not exactly understand why; for there had been enough money before. What became of it now?

She soon found out.

"I say, May," said one of the neighbour girls one evening, as she stood waiting at the door, "do you know where you father's gone? Needn't expect him home just yet. He's off up to the Half-way."

"What, the Half-way public-house?" asked May, astonished. "Oh, he don't go to the public-house, Alice. Any way, I didn't know it," she said, as it began to dawn upon her mind that perhaps this was the way in which her father spent the evenings when he left her alone.

"Don't he?" said Alice, laughing; "I don't know where else he goes to, then. You just go up and look in, and then you'll see if he's there."

This was very strange news for little May, and she was old enough to know that it was anything but good news. In her short life she had seen enough of the sadness and wretchedness that such a course would bring; and although she did not think or care whether it was right or wrong in the sight of God, she knew that when the father spent his money on himself in this way the family would want, and he himself would become unfit for the labour that brought the bread. There had not been too much money coming in before, she said, truly, to herself, for there were a great many things to buy; and on the Saturday evenings, when she used to return with her father from buying the weekly store, he had often said –

"Well, May, my girl, we've just made the two ends meet, hasn't us?"

That weekly journey had once been a very pleasant one to little May, as she had walked by her father's side along the smooth common, where the sheep peacefully nibbled the grass, or under the dark trees that bordered the high-road, until they reached the village shop. May was a sensible little maiden, and although she did not quite know it herself – and surely her father would not have acknowledged it – it was due to her good sense and management that the weekly shillings just covered their expenses; and she could quite as well have laid out the money herself as with her father's help; but it was pleasant to go with him, and have that walk back by his side in the evening's cool, as they came slowly home, carrying the large basket between them, when all the sweet nature voice seemed talking of peace and repose. For if May's affectionate little heart loved any one on earth, it was her father; very likely she herself did not know how much, but the love for him lay deep and strong.

She did not know of the great love that came down from light, and joy, and glory, to win hers. She had never listened to the gospel message, poor child; and perhaps one more ignorant than this little girl could not have been found in many places. For there was no Bible in the pretty cottage; there was no Sunday-school near, where she might learn the way to joy; and no one had taught her anything of "the good Shepherd who giveth His life for the sheep."

On this calm, sunshiny summer evening, as May sat just inside the house door waiting for her father, it was a very grave face that looked out from the rose-bushes. Alice's news had trouble her very much; and of the difference that she had noticed in her father's ways and words of late, she was obliged to own that perhaps Alice was right, and that this accounted for the lack of money on the Saturday evenings, as well as other things that she had more felt than noticed until now.

And indeed Alice's words were only too true; Thomas Wood had begun a course that could never end happily for himself or his child, as she had already begun to find out. Some of his fellow-labourers had enticed him to go with them, and to spend his evenings in what they called enjoyment, by giving the money that ought to be spent in feeding and clothing their children for what did harm to themselves; for although Farleigh did not possess many advantages, you may be sure that there was a place where men and women could ruin their bodies and souls.

And here the men would talk of the hardness of the times, and the smallness of wages; making themselves and each other discontented, and wishing they could get away to some other place where they could get more money.

So May had a long time to wait for her father this evening, all the time that the supper she had so carefully prepared was waiting near the fire, and the rows of the stocking that she was knitting were getting more and more; while he was sitting in the Half-way public-house, not thinking of his little girl at home.

At last when the shadows on the hills were becoming dark and long, and when the sun had very nearly gone down behind them, she saw him coming slowly up the slope that led to their cottage; and now that Alice's remark had made her take more notice, she saw that his face did not look so brightly or kindly at her as it had once.

But she hastened to meet him, like a sensible little woman, not saying anything about the lateness of the hour.

"Supper's ready, father," she said cheerfully, as he came near. "I've had mine, but I think yourn's almost quite hot."

"I ain't sure I want any supper," he said; "but you may bring it here, if you like."

Her father sat down inside the door, and little May soon laid out the small table, which was so neatly and carefully arranged as to have tempted him to stay at home.

"Nice evening, ain't it, Father?" said May presently; "had a good day?"

"Pretty fair," said Thomas Wood; "as good as any one in these parts, I s'pose."

"Mrs. Sykes told Alice's mother as how Farmer Coleston's men over the other way wants to have more wages, and as how he won't give no more," said May, not knowing what an interesting subject she was speaking on.

"Likely that," answered her father; "I don't suppose he will. It ain't much use to want more of what you can't get."

"It ain't right of them farmers not to give enough, is it Father?" she asked, meaning to be very sympathizing. Her father only gave a short laugh, and said nothing; so May went on with her knitting, which was growing into a nice, warm, grey stocking for her father when the winter should come on.

"Let me see, May," said her father presently, "how old be you?"

"Thirteen years old come next September," said May, decidedly.

"To think of that!" he said; "why, May, you'll be getting a young woman afore I knows it."

"What did you want to know for, Father?" asked May.

"I was a thinking. I say, May," he said again, after stopping for a few minutes, "How'd you like to see the town?"

"Depends on where it was, and what I was there for."

"Well, I've been thinking a good deal lately, and I've been taking a good deal of good advice too," said Wood, speaking slowly, and looking straight before him out towards the hills, where the trees clustered darkly in the twilight, and where the cattle were resting, quiet and content. "But what I've been thinking is this, May; and now you see I'm going to talk to you as if you was a sensible girl, which I hope you be. They tells me that a man like me could make much better wages in the town as a factory hand, and we don't get enough to make both ends meet here. I can't get along; there's a score owing at Sharp's, and there's more owing. So I've been thinking it mightn't be such a bad plan if we was just to pack up and go. We'd both get on in the town better than we does here."

"What! and go right away from here, and go for good?" asked May, astonished. And though her thoughts did not shape themselves into words, visions of the sweet home scenes that she knew so well, and regrets at the thought of leaving them, perhaps forever, passed through her mind.

"Well, yes," said her father, "I believe that's what I mean, May."

They did not say any more, but sat in the doorway, where the darkening was getting deeper. The roses shivered in the night wind and the woodbine blossoms waved gently to and fro; there were no sounds but the rustling that they made, and the faint, dreamy flowing of the river. But May did not take much heed to it all, and the darkness settled down on the hills and woods, as she sat at the cottage door, deep in her new thoughts of wonder.

Was she glad of her father's new plan? Indeed, she hardly knew; she had often wished, with a child's curiosity, to see more of the great world she lived in. Some of the neighbour girls had gone away to be servants to the nearer towns and cities, and if ever a holiday time had brought them back for a little while, May had been one of the eager listeners to their stories of city life. She had not very pleasant ideas about it; it must be lonely, she thought, living on in a strange place with strange people; and the accounts that they gave of the mistresses and the upper servants made her think that they must be very cruel. But when they spoke of the grand shops and streets – of the carriages rolling along, filled with ladies and gentlemen, with footmen behind and coachmen in front – of the parks where the trees and flowers grew, as they grow in gardens, and the stately swans sailed over the water – she thought it must be a fine thing to go to the town and to see some of these grand sights. Then how wonderful the city must be in the night-time, when, as the girls told her, "the streets was lighted up, so as to make it look most as light as day," and the beautiful things in the shop-windows sparkled and shone in the gaslight; for May only knew about the wonders of gas by name; the sweet, soft moon silvering the blue had been her lamp hitherto, and the stars were the twinkling night-lights that she had watched from her woodbine-covered window.

So her mind was very full of new thoughts and ideas. Perhaps it might not be so bad; perhaps she might like it, she thought; and at any rate, she was not going by herself; she would have her father to take care of her, just the same as in this dear little home.

But she said at length, "Father, why have you got to leave?"

"Didn't I tell you, child," he said testily; "I've got to go, and that's enough. I'm owing more than I can pay; and when we're gone, Sharp and the rest of them will have to take what they can get for the furniture."

May's heart sank low; but she only said, "Well, Father, we'll get a place in the town, then; there's little places to live in there, ain't there, as well as big ones?"

Her father fidgeted uneasily in his chair, and knocked his foot against the door-step for a little time without speaking; then he said,

"Well, May, my girl, that's the part I'm a coming to, and the part I don't know as you'll take to. Though why you shouldn't I don't know; and you may be sure, my dear, I wouldn't do nothing that wasn't for your good."

May listened in breathless expectation, wondering what would be the next surprising thing that she should hear.

So Thomas Wood continued, "You see as how it's this way, May. Long and Stone, and some of the others, has agreed to go and get factory work.

We could do that easy, you know; and they all think we should get along together; 'twould be cheaper and better every way. You see that, don't you, May?"

"Yes, Father," May answered; and then a sudden thought struck her, and she said quickly, "And where'd I be?"

"Well, you know Emma Stone, and Annie Long, and lots of the other girls, gets places; and I think you're nigh as old as them, and maybe more sensible."

May drew nearer, and gazed earnestly into her father's face, as she said softly –

"And shouldn't I be with you, Father?"

"Why, you'd be much more comfortable in some nice place, you know, May, than rubbing along with me. There's Mrs. Bond, the mistress; she's a very respectable person indeed, as I've heard say; and 'twould be a great thing to get into a respectable place to begin with. Why, who knows, but you might come some day to be a housemaid, like they have at the Manor House."

May said nothing; indeed, she had hardly heard the last part of what her father had been saying, so she sat for a long time looking out into the darkness, and wondering what strange, new thing she should hear next; and while she was thinking, she remembered that her father had spoken of some particular person, Mrs. Bond. Who could she be? And was it possible that her father could have settled with anyone already, and that she really was to be a servant in some city house? "Who's Mrs. Bond, Father?" asked May, presently.

"Well, she's sister to the lady where Emma Long is. She don't live in the same place, though. But she's a very nice person, I believe; and Emma says you'll be very comfortable; and I should see you now and again, you know."

"Then you mean, Father, that I be going out into a place. Is that what you mean, Father?"

"Well, yes, I b'lieve I do mean something like that," said May's father, after a short pause.

May said no more, but her heart sank down very low. And her father did not seem to care; a little while ago he had called her his useful little maid, and he had said so often that he did not know what he should do without her; and now his chief care seemed to be to get rid of her, so that he might be able to carry out his own plan without her. And she did love him, she did indeed; it had always been with a kind of pride that she had thought of her father, and of how different he was from the parents of the other village children. Little May was sorrow-stricken and surprised; but she was a quiet little thing, and she did not say anything just then.

Only when the time came for her to get her good-night kiss, as she wound her arm around her father's neck, a sudden thought of the dark time coming, when she should not be able to do it any more, came over her, and she laid her head on his shoulder and sobbed.

Thomas Wood was vexed. He was quite bent on carrying out his plan; but he did not want to make his little girl unhappy; and so when he had arranged for her to take a place in this lodging-house in the town, he had persuaded himself that it would be the best thing possible for her, and that of course she would like it. "Young folks always like changes, and to see the world," he said to himself.

Yet when the time had come to tell May, he had felt half afraid that she might not like it so much as he wished.

"Why, May, whatever is the matter?" he asked, as his child hung round his neck and cried. "There, I thought you'd be ever so pleased."

"Oh, Father! I shan't have no one to take care of me; no one at all."

"There, May," said her father again, "I thought you was a sensible girl. I thought you'd just like to be getting along, and earning your living."

"So I be, Father," sobbed Mary; "but I didn't think I was old enough to begin yet."

However, she did not say anything more. She went to her little room under the rafters and any tears that she shed that night were hidden by the bed-clothes. When she came down the next morning she was not crying; only if her father had watched her little face, he might have been touched by the sad expression that had fallen on it. But he did not look or notice; for he quite meant to go on as he intended at first, and he thought that May would soon get over her trouble, and get on as well as other girls.

14

And May said no more; she had sensibly made up her mind to her father's plan; but a strong feeling had come into her heart; and, perhaps, if she had been accustomed to look into it, she might have found that there was some hard sullenness there.

It would be very sad to have to say good-bye to the sweet woodbine cottage that had been her home ever since she was born; and the garden, where every summer evening she had watered her father's vegetables; and where in one corner, specially her own, she had carefully tended a moss rose tree and some geraniums. Who would tend these flowers now? And who would take care of the white cat that had been May's favourite for many a long year? For of course she could not take pussy with her; for servants in places did not generally carry cats with them.

And yet there was something rather pleasant in the sound, "a servant in a place" – something that gratified a feeling of self-importance that was in May's heart. She wondered what it would be like, this new condition of being out at service; she was not sure that she had ever seen a real servant in her working dress and occupation in her life. Emma Stone and the other girls had said something about their caps. May laughed to herself as she thought of this. "There, I wonder, shall I wear a cap?" she thought; "I should look queer, shouldn't I?"

So our little friend began building castles in the air, and, as is generally the case, they were not at all like the reality of a little maid-servant's life.

Truly it would be sad parting with her father; "but he don't seem to care," said May to herself, checking the tears that would come; "so I'd better not care neither." And then it would certainly be very nice to be in "a place." What would be her duties, and what kind of a house would her mistress's be? A real grand one, most likely, with ever so many rooms in it; and May tried to imagine a great many houses in a long row, all a great deal larger than the Half-way public-house; for that was the largest house that she had ever seen.

As Thomas Wood had really completed all his arrangements before he had said anything to his little daughter, it was not a very long time before they were ready to leave May's sweet country home, and wander away to the dull, dark city, amongst strange faces, and sights, and sounds. May was almost too busy for the greater part of this time to think much about the future that lay before her; she had her own clothes and her father's to mend neatly, and a great many other things to do, so that her little head and hands were well tired when the evening fell. The stocking had been finished, and as she packed them up with her father's other things, some tears fell into the bundle on the nicely-mended pile of clothes.

They were to go on foot to the nearest village, where the carrier's van would meet them, take them to the country town, which lay about twelve miles distant; and then a very new experience would begin for May, for they were to take the train the rest of the way to the large city which was so soon to be her home.

On the last evening before they left the village, May sat down on the door-step to take a last long look at everything, and to say good-bye to it all, as she said to herself. She could hardly have expressed all the strange, new feelings that came into her heart as she watched the bright river flowing down into the valley, and the green trees sheltering and clothing the soft outline of the hilly range; and then her eye rested on each lane and road, each little dell and hollow, that she knew almost as well as she knew her own cottage home; and she began to wonder, would she ever see it again, and if she did, what would happen between. It was very strange and rather sad, and as May thought of it all, tears filled her eyes, and her head bent down on her lap.

Presently a clear, bright voice called her name, "Well, May, I've come to say good-bye."

She looked up quickly, and saw that it was one of her friends who lived near. "Oh, Alice! I didn't know it was you."

"Well, 'tis, but it won't be me long; for mother only let me run in for a minute. Talk about hard work! It's me that has that, and no play, neither. May, I wish I was you."

"I don't then," said May.

"Why, you'll have ever so much fun; 'twill be your own fault if you don't. I dare say your missus will let you out of an evening sometimes; and then just fancy all you'll see – shops and the lovely things in them, and all lights up so grand."

"I don't think I care so very much," said May, gently.

"And then, fancy how grand you'll be. Dear, I s'pose if I was to come along in a month's time where you'll be, you wouldn't know me at all; and if I was to come up to the house where you're to be, and give a little knock, such a grand young woman would come to open the door, with her hair all done up town fashion."

May smiled at her friend's fancies; but it was not altogether a happy smile.

"But what are you going to be, May?" asked Alice. "I think I'd like to know if I was you."

"I don't know," May answered with a sigh; "I suppose I shall have to do what I'm told."

"That's my business too," said Alice. "Well, I've got something for you. Look here, it's not quite new; but ain't it pretty?"

She showed her a book marker, with a bright blue ribbon; and the words that were marked on the cardboard were, "Come unto Me."

Very little either of these two girls knew about those blessed words then, and May did not know what a voice their sweetness would be to her heart's depths some day.

"Oh, that is nice!" she said. "And to think of your giving of this to me; that was kind, Alice. I'll keep it all my life, and think of you."

Alice looked pleased.

"'Twas my cousin's school teacher gave it to her," she said, "and she let me have it." And she told me the words there was, 'Come unto Me.' You mind them, May, 'cause you can't read yet, can you?"

"No," said May. "Father says I hasn't had time to learn, but maybe I might get time in the town, if there was anyone to teach me there."

"I dare say there's lots to teach, but I don't know about the time; I shouldn't think you'd have too much of that. But I must go. Good-bye, May; give me a good kiss, and don't forget me, even if you do get genteel."

When Alice was gone, May looked at her little gift again. It was very pretty, she thought, and it was almost the only present that she had ever had. Then she said the words over to herself again, that she might not forget them. She wondered who had said them; they sounded so kind, she thought. She did not know it was the gracious Son of God, whose arms of love were even then held out towards the wanderers straying on the earth, and nearing every day a land which to them must be one of darkness, if they had not answered the voice that calls to eternal love and care.

CHAPTER 2

THE JOURNEY

It was a long and wearying walk that had lain before May and her father on that sunny June morning, when they had left the old home, looking just as sweet and as bright as ever. The jessamine stars had seemed to look sadly in answer to May's tearful gaze, and the roses had nodded good-bye as they bent in the summer wind, while the woodbine clusters had seemed to cling more firmly to the cottage, as if they were saying, "We will take care of the old place, though you desert it."

The neighbours had looked out of their doors and windows to see them as they passed up the hill that led into the main road, and some of the girls that they met going to their daily toil had been disposed to look with envying eyes on the lot that they thought lay before May, but to which she herself looked forward with very mingled feelings.

It had seemed so strange to pass all the old familiar places one after the other, and to feel that she was leaving them all behind; every step was leading her into a new and untried world, which might be such a strange place for her; "but anyway,

I shall be in the same town with father," she said to herself, as she took hold of his strong, brown hand, to check the little starting feeling of fear that arose.

The journey in the carrier's van had come next, and they had taken their places in the large red and yellow vehicle that was awaiting its burden of country people outside the inn. This journey was not nearly so pleasant as May had fancied it would have been in the old days, when she had watched the van passing along the high road, and she had wished to be inside. She had her wish now, and she found that it was very hot and uncomfortable to be seated in there.

Her father had found acquaintances in some of the other travelers; and while he was engaged with them, his little girl was left to amuse herself with the new scenes and places through which they were passing.

By and by they reached the country town; and although it was a very quiet place, and there were not many people coming and going, the bustle and activity seemed very great to May, and she was gazing all around with surprise and admiration. It was a pretty place, and in the principal street a newly-built drinking fountain was flowing in the sunlight, and throwing the light drops over the carved figures and stonework, that seemed so beautiful.

It was evening when they reached the great city. Very strange had been May's feelings when the train, in which they had taken their places, had moved out of the station and was swiftly passing on its way; then, when the darkness of the tunnel had suddenly come on, and, all unknown to May, the bright sunlight had gone, it was with a little scream of fear that she had clung to her father, not knowing what had caused the darkness. It was frightful, certainly, when, in the sudden darkness, the loud rumbling of the train had become more loud; and the carriage lamp above had shone down on a pale, scared little face.

But now they had arrived at their journey's end – the place where May knew that she was to spend a very long time perhaps. It was a bewildering scene for our little country maiden, as she stood on the large, crowded platform, where the shouting and bustling, the farewells and greetings, the rolling of the luggage trucks, and all the various sights and sounds that pass in a city railway station were going on. How very large it looked, and what a number of people were there!

Her little box and bundle were soon found, and when her father had gathered his own possessions, they soon made their way out of the station into the street.

And now indeed May might open her eyes and look around as they passed along. The daylight had not quite faded away, and in the country people had not begun to light their candles yet; but here in the city the streets were one blaze of bright gaslight, and it seemed to her as if all the people were in one vast hurry and bustle. Where could they all be going, and what could they all be doing? Why were the drivers all driving so fast? While the foot-passengers seemed hurrying after one another, as if something very important was drawing them on. Then, how high the houses were, and the streets were so long; very long indeed they seemed to May's weary little legs, as she passed along the way by her father's side.

Number 47, Hartly Street, was their destination, and heartily she was wishing that they might soon reach it. A friendly cab-driver at the station had directed them; but as they passed through street after street, and still it did not appear, May began to be sadly afraid that they must have come the wrong way, or that amongst the number of names that they had seen printed up her father had missed seeing this one.

"Oh, Father!" she said at length with a weary sigh, "ain't we 'most there?"

"We ought to be, that's for sure. Hope we've come all right. 'Most tired, May?"

"Yes, I be, Father. What kind of a looking place is it?"

"They told me 'twas a long, dark street, with all the houses looking alike," her father said.

"Dear; I think we've passed a lot like that already."

"Yes, but this here Hartley Street looks different from the rest. I should know it, if it looks the same as it did long ago when I was here. And I do b'lieve May," he said, as they came to the end of the street through which they had been passing, and were entering into another, "I do believe that this is it."

It proved that he was right. "Hartley Street" was printed in white letters on the end where they were; but this was only number one, and there was forty-six houses to be passed before they should reach Mrs. Bond's, which was the name of May's new mistress.

The house in Hartley Street was a large lodging-house; so you may imagine that both the mistress and her maids had quite enough every day to occupy their time and attention, especially as there was only one other servant kept, besides the little girl who had just left her country home to enter on this busy life of labour. The place that May was expected to fill would be rather difficult to describe, because it consisted in doing what the others did not do, and in being ready for it. However, if she had been a little older and stronger, it would not have been such a very hard place for any one accustomed to town life, for neither Mrs. Bond nor her other servant could be called unkind; and although the mistress herself was careless and unfeeling, May found a friend in Ellen, the other servant.

At length they reached the door, and tired as she was, May looked curiously up at the house where she was to live. It was, as were all the others, tall and dark and gloomy looking; even the windows had no cheery look about them, for the shutters were shut, and if there was light within, it was not seen.

A flight of stone steps led up to the door, and when they had climbed there, and were resting for a moment, May's father pointed to the clean brass plate and door handle, and with a quiet smile he said,

"See that, May? Wonder who keeps 'em clean now? I daresay that'll be your work one day."

But in some way these words fell with a very cold weight on May's heart; she had been feeling very cheerless indeed, and these words of her father seemed to remind her so forcibly of the days that were coming, and to bring a picture of her lonely life of toil before her; she burst into tears, perhaps partly because she was so very tired.

"O May, child!" said her father, vexed and astonished, "why, whatever is the matter? There, don't cry; don't let 'em see you crying the first thing when they comes," he said anxiously, as the sound of footsteps on the other side of the door could be heard coming nearer.

May dried her tears hardly in time; for the door opened, and a bright, rather sharp-looking girl, some years older than herself, stood before them.

"Oh," she said, "I suppose you're the new girl that Missus has been expecting. Well, come along."

"Father, shall I say good-bye now?" asked May, her lips trembling again.

"You can wait, if you like, Sir, in the passage," said Ellen, as she took May's bundle from her hand. "Your little girl feels strange, maybe, and I daresay she'd like to see you again, after she's spoke to the mistress."

25

"I think, maybe, I will," said Wood. May hardly noticed the way by which she was being led; only it seemed very long, as she followed her companion through a passage, then down a long flight of stairs, and through another passage, until they reached a door covered with green baize, where Ellen knocked as she said, "This is the mistress's room."

Some one inside said, "Come in;" and then as they entered, and May dropped her respectful curtsey, she looked timidly at her new mistress; though the gaslight was so bright, that at first she could hardly see her.

She was a gaily-dressed person, of about forty years old. She was sitting at the table beneath the gaslight, with a desk and a pile of papers before her; and as May entered the room, she said, "Good evening. May. That's your name, isn't it – May Wood? Well, I suppose you know all that you will be expected to do here. You look rather small; but if you make up your mind to work hard, I daresay you will do."

"Yes, ma'am," said Mary, curtseying again.

"You see it's mostly as a help I got my sister to engage you. You will have to work downstairs mostly, and sometimes upstairs, when Ellen is busy, and with the lodgers, who are not so particular."

"Yes, ma'am," said May again.

"I think she'd better have something to eat and go to bed, now," suggested Ellen; "she's come a long way."

"Yes; I suppose she had," said Mrs. Bond. "And then you make haste down, Ellen; there's plenty for you to do, at any rate."

"Yes; that you may be sure there is," said Ellen, when they were outside the door. "And you'll find that out pretty soon, too. But I won't make you downhearted the first evening. What a funny name you have. Whatever made 'em call you May?"

"Well, you see, my real name's Maria; but when I was little I couldn't say it; so I called myself May, and mother said 'twas prettier."

"You haven't got a mother now, then," said Ellen. "No more have I, and my father ain't much good to me. Oh, and I forgot! Here's yours been waiting all this time to say good-bye to you."

When May really had to say good-bye to her father, she clung round his neck with a passionate strength, and it seemed as if she could not tear herself away. It was a very sad farewell; for she felt in her heart that the only person in the world who cared about her was giving her up; and in the weakness of her loneliness she cried and sobbed.

And there was no one to whisper a word to her about the kind Friend who loves as no one else can; and she could not hear the voice that was saying, "As one whom his mother comforteth, so will I comfort you." Her mother was dead, and her father was leaving her; but there was a loving One near, who had taken little children up in His arms and blessed them; and He was saying, "Come unto me."

"Oh, Father! Whatever shall I do without you, all by myself? Need I stay, Father?"

"There, don't take on so," said her father. In his heart he was almost sorry that they had ever come; but he knew that it was too late now. "Why, May, you know you must; and I'll come and see you as often as ever I can. You'll like it well, by and by; and you'll be right glad you came. Come, cheer up; good-bye, my little darling."

May's tears only came faster at these endearing words; and still she stayed with her arms around her father's neck; and the sobs that he felt as she clung to him touched his heart more than he let her know. But May suddenly checked herself as she thought that she heard the mistress's door opening below; and loosening her arms from her father's neck, she said –

"Good-bye, father dear; maybe you'd better go now. I think I hear some one coming."

Ellen, the other servant, was a kind-hearted girl, and she pitied the poor little stranger, who had evidently been so unaccustomed to any place save her own native home. When her father was gone she gave her a good supper, and insisted that she should eat; for she saw that May was weak and weary.

Then she led her up to a very small room at the top of the house, which they were to share. What a long way it seemed to May before they reached it; perhaps she had never gone upstairs in her life before, for their cottage home was only of one story. When they had reached the first landing she stopped and asked, as she looked at the doors around, did either of these belong to the room where she was to sleep. Ellen looked astonished.

"Dear me," she said; "why these is the lodgers' drawing-rooms. Did you ever think you was going to be there?"

"Is it much higher?" asked May. "Why I think we'll be in the clouds soon."

"I don't know about that," said Ellen; "but I'll tell you we sleeps up at the very tip top of the house. I know I'm glad I do; and so'll you be. It's away from the mistress, and that's a good thing."

"But why?" asked May.

"Well, I suppose, if you're not particularly fond of a person, you don't want to be nearer to them than you can help, do you?"

The room upstairs was a very small one, and it was not at all so clean as May's own little room at home had been; but at first May thought it had a magnificent appearance, for there were several pieces of furniture in it that Mrs. Bond had put there when they became too old to adorn her drawing-room and parlour downstairs. Over the little fireplace was a gilt-framed looking-glass, and although there was a large crack right across it, and the gilt moulding was blackened and broken, May could not understand why her mistress should give such furniture for her servants' room. What must her own be! And what was inside the best bedrooms where the lodgers slept, downstairs! She had never seen such a looking-glass before; for there had not been one of any sort in their cottage; and so May had grown up, really hardly knowing what kind of a face she had. Perhaps this was just as well, because it was a pretty one; and some little girls, with far less cause, have been foolish enough to let their appearance occupy a great deal of their thoughts, who had not May's golden hair and sweet blue eyes.

"Well," said Ellen, "you do seem taken with that glass! You won't have time to be looking at yourself every day, I can tell you."

"I wasn't looking at myself," said May, blushing."

"Weren't you? I thought that was what people looked in glasses for generally. Or perhaps it's the beautiful cobwebs on it you're admiring," said Ellen, laughing. "But now I must go. Good night; I hope you'll be rested to-morrow."

When Ellen had gone, and her quick, hard footsteps had ceased to sound down the long flight of stairs, May sat down on the floor and buried her face in the bed-clothes. First she began to think; but she felt very confused and bewildered still. Could it have been really only that morning that she awoke in the old home and that her eyes had rested on the things that she had seen ever since she could remember? Was it really only that day that they had climbed up the Half-way hill for the last time; that they had been in the carrier's van, and that she and her father had sat side by side in that wonderful train? May could not realize her new position at all; she could only feel that she was very, very lonely, and that everything was strange and new.

Presently she went to the window; and when her eyes were accustomed to the darkness without, it was a very different scene from the old one at home that she saw; her window looked on the backs of the other houses, and very dismal it was – dreary, black-looking houses and windows shadowed around, one looking much the same as another; it was all so different from the sweet home prospect, where the soft hills were covered by the trees, and the little white cottages arose here and there, and far apart.

But when she looked up to the clear, bright sky, there were just the same stars that she had been accustomed to seeing; there was the Great Bear (though May did not know it by that name) stretching across the blue, and the seven clustering stars, to which she and her companions had given names of their own. May stayed a long time looking out, while her thoughts were straying far away, and the strange, lonely feeling was growing stronger, until she went back to her place by the bedside, and sobbed bitterly there, and alone. Poor little thing! She was very young to begin the battle of life; and she could not help thinking, that perhaps, if her mother had lived, it would never have been as it was now. "Oh, Mother, Mother," she whispered to herself, "I wish you hadn't died! Oh, I wish father hadn't begun going to the Half-way!" And the familiar name brought back the lonely feeling that made her tears flow afresh.

When Ellen came up to bed, she found her sitting there, quite still and pale; for her crying was over now.

"What, not in bed!" she said. "Well, I never did. Why I thought you were tired! I do believe you've been crying all the time; and I'll tell you what – you had better not; it's no good, you know. Why, if I was to cry about everything I didn't like, I'd be crying all day too."

May only gave a very deep sigh; but she said nothing.

"And there's another thing," said Ellen presently, "you ain't so badly off, after all; for you've got your father. And I know I'd be glad if my father was worth caring about."

"Oh, Ellen!" said May, in a very shocked tone of voice.

"It's true though," Ellen answered, bitterly.

She would not let May sit up any longer; she lifted her up from her seat on the floor, and helped her to undress, her kindness nearly bringing May's tears back again; for this rough girl had some soft feelings, after all.

"Do you know," she said, stooping over May, as she lay in bed, "I had a little sister once, and you mind me of her a bit. She had hair like yours. And 'twas father's ways killed her," she added bitterly.

"And where did she go when she died?" asked May, eagerly.

"Why to heaven of course. Where should she go to?"

"Does every one go to heaven?" asked May again.

"I don't know. I suppose people that hasn't done any particular harm goes there."

It was not very long before May was asleep; but her dreams were very strange and confused that night; pictures of her old home-life, and her varied journey mixed themselves with curious impressions of the days that were coming. Ellen did not awaken her very early the next morning; for she had taken a fancy to the stranger girl, and she meant to be as kind to her as she could.

CHAPTER 3

MAY'S TOWN HOME

Mrs. Bond's house in Hartley Street was a very large one; and except the underground part, and the small garret where her servants slept, it was entirely given up to her lodger. So there was quite enough for them to do, and more than enough, they very often thought.

Very tired and sleepy little May often felt, as she followed Ellen up to the top of the house in the evening; and when the morning came, and she knew that she must begin over again, it seemed to be a very short time since she had gone to sleep. And she was quite at home now in those grand rooms, that had once seemed to be so magnificent; she had learned to dust the ornaments on the mantel-pieces, which in the beginning she had been almost afraid to touch; and her arms were becoming accustomed to sweeping the rooms, and shaking the door-mats; very hard work she found it at first, and her back ached painfully. There were very few moments in the day that were not occupied in one way or

34

another; there was always something to be done, and most of the running and fetching fell to May's lot. So that, except for the bustle that she heard all the day outside, and the little glimpses that she caught of the city now and again, when she was sent to the neighbouring streets, she did not know much of the town.

One evening, when there was not so much business as usual to be done, Mrs. Bond told her two maids that they might have the rest of the day to do as they pleased; and then Ellen said she would take May to the park.

Ellen evidently considered this was a great treat; but May's admiration and surprise were a great deal more excited by the streets through which they passed on their way there. Her companion could hardly make her come on as they passed some of the shops; she wanted to know the names of the things that she saw, and what were their uses.

"And, oh Ellen," she said, "do you think I'd ever be able to buy any of them things, when I get my first quarter's money?"

"I don't think you'll get any quarter's money, if you stay loitering here all night," said Ellen crossly; "for we shall be late. Do come on, child."

So May tore herself away from the beautiful things that she saw, and followed Ellen, until they reached the park. It was not such a very wonderful place, after all, she thought; and she was not nearly so pleased and surprised as Ellen had intended that she should be. May thought that the park was a little bit like her own old home, only not nearly so nice; and yet it was not like the country, because of all the gaily dressed people who were thronging there. It seemed like the town and the country mixed up together. So that decidedly the beauties of the streets were what May had admired in their evening's expedition.

"There, Ellen!" she said, when they were once more in their little garret room, "they was beautiful, them things. I wonder shall I ever be able to buy any. You've been a long time in service; have you got any?"

"I didn't never buy any," said Ellen. "I've got something else to do with my money. I've got something though, that I daresay you'd think mighty fine. 'Twas given to me."

"Oh, do show me!" May asked eagerly. So Ellen went to her black box, that stood in the window, and took out something that shone in the candlelight; and brought it over for May to see. It was a gilt brooch and earrings, ornamented with green glass. May thought they were gold and diamonds, and she quite satisfied Ellen by her admiration.

"Well, that was a present!" she said. "I never had but one present in all my life, and that was gave me just before I came away."

"What was that?" asked Ellen.

"A book-marker." Ellen laughed.

"Don't laugh," said May, "and I'll show it to you. I want to know if you know what the words mean."

So May took out her one present, and showed it to Ellen. "I know what the words is," she said; "the girl that gave it to me told me, and I remember."

"What, can't you read yourself then?" said Ellen.

May looked rather ashamed, as she said, "No, a good many people in our country can't read. My father can, though; and he said maybe he'd teach me when the winter evenings came; but you see we came away before that."

"I'll teach you, if you like," said Ellen, suddenly. "Why shouldn't I? I've got a spelling book with the alphabet in it."

"Oh, you are nice!" said May, joyfully. "There, I thought someway I should learn, when I got to the town. And I know the letters already."

"Do you?" said Ellen. "Oh, then you'll not be very long learning to spell out the easy parts. You'd best begin with the Bible, when you know a little; that's easy, some parts."

"The Bible," said May. "I don't know much about that; but I want to ever so much. I don't think that we had a Bible in our home."

"I've got one; 'twas my little sister's. And as you're like her, you may have it to read out of when you know how; that is you may if you want to."

"Ellen," said May, "do you know I wish I was your real sister. It seems I've got nobody to belong to now; for father never comes nigh me now."

37

"Poor little soul," said Ellen kindly; "maybe he can't, you know. But you ain't so badly off here."

"Oh no; I ain't, I suppose. Only sometimes when I think of how it used to be before my mother died; why, she and father hadn't nobody but me. And mother, how she used to fret if I were ill, or if my head ached. Missus don't care a bit."

"No, that she don't," said Ellen. "I believe she'd be right glad of any bit of pain we had, if it brought another shilling into her pocket."

"But come," said Ellen, "you haven't showed me your present."

So May brought out her bookmarker from its covering of white paper. "Now," she said, "that's 'Come unto me,' ain't it? But I want to know who says it."

"Why, don't you know that, child?" asked Ellen. "Why them's Bible words. God says it, I s'pose."

"God!" May asked, surprised. "Why, God lives in heaven. How could He?"

"How can I tell?" said Ellen, rather crossly. "I ain't a minister."

"No, but do tell me; I do so want to know. I always wanted to know about them words. What does God want us to come to Him for?"

"Dear, how you bother. Teacher used to say, 'twas to be saved. Now, don't you ask me one more word about it," said Ellen, turning away very decidedly, and busying herself about the room.

But May wanted very much to ask more. Was it not sad that there was no one to tell her? No one to say, "The Lord Jesus wants you, little May. He says, 'Come unto me, all ye that labour and are heavy laden, and I will give you rest.'" Was it not a pity, that when there was no earthly father to cherish her, she did not feel the strong kind arm of everlasting love thrown around her, and that her lonely, loving heart could not sing for joy in a glad song. "Unto Him that loveth us, and hath washed us from our sins in His own blood." You see how very, very ignorant she was; and that there are a great many children, not half her age, who know a great deal more than she did.

"Ellen," said May, by and by, after the candle had been put out, and they were both in bed; she was almost afraid to ask the question, only she wanted so very much to know; "Just let me ask you this one question, and I won't tease you no more. Does God mean everybody, or only very good people?"

"If anybody else was to talk that way to me, I'd not answer them," said Ellen, "especially as I don't know. And I don't see what you've got to do with such things either. My teacher used to say, He came to save the lost, and I suppose that doesn't mean very good people. I suppose they've got to be sorry, though; and I know I ain't very sorry. Now be quiet and go to sleep, there's a good child."

But May did not go to sleep so very soon that night, for she was thinking. She knew that there was a heaven and a hell; that there was a great God who had made everything, and who lived far away from here, in some place where she had never been; but no one had told her the story of God's great love, and her ear had never listened to a voice speaking of the life and death of Him who, "though He was rich, yet for your sakes He became poor."

May wondered what would happen to her if she should die, as her mother had done; but she did not like to think of it, and the thought of the green grass growing above her, and the life of nature singing over her grave, would bring a cold shudder to her heart; for she knew no bright thoughts of being "forever with the Lord;" and she had no glad confidence that He would take care of her forever.

Little May knew that if God only meant "good people," when He said, "Come unto me," that she was not invited.

"I ain't so very bad, for sure," she said to herself; "but I ain't good enough for God, because God knows everything. Maybe God meant He'd save the people that hadn't done anything particularly bad. I wish I knew. I wish Ellen would tell me. I'm sure I'd tell her if she wanted to know, and I did." May sighed, and it was a weary sigh.

A few mornings after this, when Mrs. Bond's little servant-maid was busy with the house-work, a ring sounded from the front door. Ellen was passing with a tray to one of the upstairs rooms. "Run, May," she said, "and see who it is. It's only a ring, so it's no one to come in, I daresay."

May ran quickly to the door, and when she saw her father standing there, the pleasure that danced in her loving little heart showed itself in her bright face, and sounded in the glad ring of her voice, as she threw her arms around him and said –

"Oh, Father, is it you? There, I thought the ring had a nice kind of sound, when I heard it."

This was only the second time that May had seen her father since they had come to live in the town.

"Well, my girl," he said, after they had talked for a little while, "I suppose you are getting on quite comfortable. Do you think you'll suit?"

"Oh, I s'pose so," said May, with a little sigh. "I s'pose I'm as well here as anywhere else, 'cept at home. I like the other girl here, and she's very kind to me."

"What does the mistress say to you?" asked her father.

"Oh, she don't say nothing particular. Ellen don't like her at all, and I don't mind her either way. And how are you getting on, Father?"

"Very bad, very bad indeed, my dear," her father answered. "I think I have come to the wrong place. Long and Stone has gone on to the next town; they say there's no getting on here at all."

A sudden thought flashed across May's mind.

"Oh, Father," she said, "if you can't get on here, and you could at home just, wouldn't it be better to go back home? And you know," she said, thinking that now she had found a strong argument with her father, "if you was to go home now, Father,

41

after having lived such a long time in the city, 'course they'd be ever so glad to have you back, and maybe they'd give you more wages."

"What a silly child you be, May," said her father, crossly. I wish you'd give over always a wanting to go back home. I told you we couldn't go, and I tell you so again."

Little May said nothing; but she looked very sad as she asked, "What be you going to do then, Father?"

"Well, you see," he said, in a hesitating voice, "I don't see much of you now-a-days, not as much as I'd like, you know; your missus wouldn't like it; and when you are in a place you must mind her. And so I was thinking – just thinking, you know – if I was to go where Long and Stone is gone, it would be much better for both of us. And then maybe soon I might get enough money for you to come to the same place."

May's father did not look at her as he was speaking, or else he would have seen an expression on his little daughter's face that was not very often there. May was not only saddened by these tidings that her father had brought, but the feelings that were in her heart just then were angry and bitter ones. She did not speak for a moment or two, and then she said –

"I don't care then, Father. I don't b'lieve you care a bit for me. I b'lieve you're just getting like Ellen's father, who killed her little sister; and you wouldn't be sorry if you heard I was drowned to-morrow."

And May burst into a passion of angry tears.

"There," said Thomas Wood, soothingly; "now don't, my dear; you mustn't be silly, you know. Why, May, I used to think you was quite sensible."

"And I us'n't never to think you'd go on this way, Father," said May, still crying bitterly. "Oh, if mother hadn't died you wouldn't, know you wouldn't."

May still sobbed on, while her father appeared to be very busily employed in tracing the carvings that were upon the hall door. He had quite made up his mind to leave the town before he had come to tell his child about it; but selfish as he was, he did not like to see her grief, and he wanted to leave her more happy and cheerful than she was now. If he loved any one at all in the world, she was the one; and he persuaded himself that it would be the best thing for her as well as for himself. May was the first to speak after some little time.

"Well," she said, "I suppose if you've got to go, it's the best thing. Am I to live all my life with Mrs. Bond?"

"All your life, child," laughed her father. "I don't know as how either you or her would be agreeable to that. Why, my dear, I daresay I'll be back again very soon; any way, if you're not comfortable, just let me know. And as to living all your life here, you've got a long life before you; and as you've begun to move so early, I shouldn't wonder if you moved a bit more afore you're much older. Cheer up, May; a great many girls would be as glad as anything at the change you've got."

May smiled, but it was a sad little smile.

"Well, I mustn't stay standing here," she said; "so good-bye, Father."

Her lips trembled as she said good-bye; and when her father put his arms around her neck and kissed her, her tears broke forth afresh.

"Oh, Father, I can't help it, you know," she said; "you be the only one that belongs to me. And I do love you ever so much, though I spoke cross just now."

"There, my dear," he said, "we'll be all right again some day, I daresay; and I won't forget my little May."

When he had gone, May rushed upstairs to the top of the house; and unheeding that her business was standing still all this time, she ran quickly into her own little room, and threw herself down on the bed in a torrent of bitter sobbing.

She was a very lonely little child, and there was no one to tell her that she need not be alone; her heart was very bitter indeed, and she did not know about the One who has borne our griefs and carried our sorrows. She had seen her earthly home broken up, and her heart had not found its gladness in looking forward to the many mansions where the kind Master has gone to prepare a place for His own.

CHAPTER 4

SOMETHING ABOUT JOY

A great many people were constantly coming and going in Mrs. Bond's house; for there were many rooms in it, and the visitors who came did not usually stay very long in the city.

May did not in general take much interest in the people who lodged there; indeed, she had not very much to do with them; for it was Ellen's duty to wait at table and to answer the bells, which they both thought were rung so very often.

But the large drawing-room had been vacant for some little time, and Mrs. Bond was beginning to be uneasy; she generally had very little difficulty in letting her rooms; and now no one had taken them for nearly a week. So when, on the Saturday afternoon, a cab drove up to the door, piled very high indeed with different sorts of luggage, there was at least one person in the house who was very glad to see it; but when Mrs. Bond looked more closely from her window, and saw three little heads peering from inside the cab, and one brown-haired boy sitting beside the driver, she was not quite so cheerful as she had been at first; for she had a great objection to children in every way, but especially as lodgers; for she said that they were more plague than profit, and "always in the way." However, she weighed the for and against of the circumstances in her own mind, and at length came to the conclusion that they should be admitted, especially as the lady said that very probably they would not be long in the town.

For they had just come away from their home in the country, which was now given up – a sweet, bright home it had been, where all the children were born, and where the nature sights and sounds had surrounded them hitherto; it was in this place that their gentle, delicate mother had spent many peaceful years, and, as she now said to herself, she had made her heart's home there, where it might not rest.

But now her husband's fortune had been taken away – not by his own fault, but through the treachery of a man whom he had trusted; and when that was gone, he saw that they could no longer live in the home that she had thought would always be theirs, and that the hills and trees which had cradled her children's baby lives would not shelter their growing youth from the strife of sin and sorrow. She was forgetting that God knows best, and that He could arrange in His own way what was the safest and the happiest for her and hers. So when one evening, after she had spent a time of anxious suspense and trembling, fearing, and yet hardly daring to think of what she feared, her husband came home and told her that everything was really gone, and that it would be quite necessary for them and their children to leave their home, and to go away from England altogether, she felt first as if she could not do it, and the dreary aching wore at her heart when she thought of the wild, lonely, unknown land where they must go – over the sea; for her husband had told her that now Australia must be their home; and as he spoke hopefully of the future, and said "After all, you know, darling, we may find as happy a home there as here," she felt that she could not say so.

But God had taught her a great deal since then; so that now, as she was speaking to Mrs. Bond about the rooms, and saying that they would probably want them only for a few days, as they were soon leaving England for Australia, only a faint shadow passed over her sweet, pale face, which gave a depth to the softness that was there.

May soon began to take an interest in their new lodger; and while Ellen seemed to agree with her mistress that children gave a great deal of trouble, May was very glad they were there; and when she was sent into the room where they were, she was always more pleased than when she was told to answer any of the other bells; and this was very often; for as Mrs. Bond did not consider Mrs. Vernon and her family very profitable lodgers, she was not so particular about them as about some of the others, and it was often found that Ellen was too busy to wait at their table.

The little Vernons were inclined to be amused at their small servant; but she did not know this as she waited in the room, attending only very partially to her business, for she was a great deal more interested in their conversation. It gave a sad feeling to her heart, which she could hardly understand, to see all these children so happy together, and to notice the fond way in which their mother cared for them, and took notice of anything that they did and said. Charlie and Carrie, the two eldest, were full of hopes and plans about their new home across the sea, and little Ernest and Nellie knew that they were going with their father and mother, and that was the chief care with them.

"'Twould be queer, too, if that lady and gentleman was to go away and leave all them children behind," sighed May to herself. And then she thought that this was just what her own father had done, and that it must be a fine thing to be a gentleman's child.

One day the two younger children had been out with their mother, and as May opened the hall door for them, she noticed that Ernest carried a thin, flat parcel in his hand, which he held very carefully.

"Now, Ernie," said little Nellie, "let me carry it upstairs. You know you've carried it all the way from the shop."

"Oh, but Nellie," Ernest remonstrated, "that was because you did not want to carry it before.

And just now is when I want to have it, of course. That wouldn't be fair. Would it, Mamma?"

Mrs. Vernon did not say anything, but Nellie looked very much put out as she said, "I would have carried it all the way, if I thought you would not let me have it now."

"Oh, Nellie, how selfish you are!" said Ernest hotly. "I wouldn't mind giving it to you, if you were not so cross about everything."

Ernest looked up just then into his mother's face, and saw that she was looking at him; then she bent down, and said in a whisper that was only meant for him, "Don't you know, darling, who said, 'Lovest thou Me?' I don't think that is the way to show we love Him, is it?"

Little Ernest was a follower of the Lord Jesus, and though he often failed and did wrong, and pleased himself, yet his mother knew that he really did love the kind Saviour, and that he had given his heart to Him; so now she anxiously watched to see whether he would give up his own way.

She had not to wait very long. Ernest looked at the parcel, and then he looked at his little sister's grieved face, and said suddenly.

"Very well, Nellie dear, then you shall have it; only take care of the edges."

When May went into the drawing-room again, she found the mystery of the thin parcel explained; for at each end of the mantelpiece were two large white pieces of cardboard, on each of which something was printed in plain blue letters;

and although she had had several reading lessons from Ellen, she did no know what the blue letters spelt; only something familiar seemed to strike her in the beginning of one of them. By and by it came into her mind that they must be the same words that were on her own little book-marker up stairs, the words that she so well remembered; but there must be more here than those three short words.

How she would like to know the rest! She wondered if Master Ernest would tell her; she should so very much like to know.

Presently May thought she would see if the three words were really the same; so, as no one was calling her, and as there were no busy sounds downstairs, she quickly mounted to her own little room, up the flight of stairs which had long ceased to seem so wonderfully high, and brought down her one treasure.

Yes, she really thought the words were the same, but what the rest of the sentence was she wished in vain to find out. She was so deeply considering this that she did no hear a little soft footstep treading on the carpet near where she stood; and presently a silvery childish voice, soft and clear as it was, made her start violently, as little Nellie said,

"What can you be looking at, May?"

"Oh, Miss Nellie, please," said May, blushing a deep red, "I was only looking at them things."

"What have you got in your hand?" asked Nellie.

"What can you be looking at, May?" said little Nellie.—
Page 50.

"That's my book-marker, Miss; and I was thinking the words there looked the same as these, only there's ever so much more. I did so want to know what the rest was. I suppose you couldn't tell me, Miss?"

"Of course I could!" said Nellie indignantly. "Why, it's as easy as it can be. It's 'Come unto Me, all ye that labour and are heavy laden, and I will give you rest.'"

May looked up eagerly as the words came; but they were spoken so very quickly that she could hardly understand.

"If you just wouldn't mind saying it again, Miss Nellie," she said.

"How funny you are!" said Nellie. "Oh, yes, I'll say it again, if you like." And this time she spoke more slowly, and as if the words had struck her own heart, as not fit to be hurried over as any others would be.

"Who says it?" asked May presently.

"Why, don't you know that?" said Nellie, astonished. "God says it; at least the Lord Jesus Christ does. He said it when He was on the earth."

"Oh, dear! I wish He was here now!"

"Why?" asked Nellie very gravely, and looking curiously at the little servant girl, who seemed to have feelings that she had never known.

"Because then I'd go to Him," said May.

Nellie seemed uneasy, and as if she did not quite know what to say.

"I think," she said presently, "perhaps mamma could talk to you better than I can. I think you had better talk to her, or to Ernest. Oh, here is Ernest coming! Ernie," she said, running to him, "do you know May wants to know about my text; and I don't think she knows anything about anything. Do you, May?"

"No, Miss, I don't think I do know much. But then I hadn't nobody to teach me. I do know a little about the Bible though, and I've just begun to learn to read."

"Oh, dear, dear!" said thoughtless Nellie, skipping out of the room, "I knew how to read ever so long ago, and I'm not nearly as old as you are now."

"What did you want to know, May?" asked Ernest a little timidly.

Ernest loved the Lord Jesus Christ with a true heart answer to the greatest of all loves, and it was a deep wish with him to do something to please the Lord.

Sometimes, when he spoke to his mother about the future which he hoped lay before him, he would speak of himself as a messenger of that great love, a servant of the One of whom he had already learnt to say, "Whose I am, and whom I serve;" and he hoped that God might one day call him to carry His glorious message of joy to the distant ones who had never heard it. Ernest knew that to serve the Lord Jesus Christ meant to follow Him, and to do the work that He gave.

"I don't know 'xactly what I wanted to ask, Master Ernest," said May, "Miss Nellie told me what the words was."

"Why, you know," said Ernest, speaking slowly as he began, "it was our Saviour who said that, and I thought perhaps, May," he said, "that you wanted to go to Him. You know, if you do, He would make you so happy. He would make you happy in heaven forever."

"I should like to go to heaven," said May softly. "I was only a thinking of it the other night. I haven't done anything particular bad."

"It doesn't matter," said Ernest; "if you've ever done one bad thing, you can't go to heaven. I mean, you can't get yourself in there."

May looked earnestly at him; for he seemed to be saying terrible things; and yet surely he must have done some wrong things in all his life; though he certainly was one of the best-behaved boys that she had ever seen.

"I thought maybe," she said, "that if I was to ask God every day, and ever so often, to let me go to heaven when I died, He'd let me in."

"Why, May," said Ernest with a happy smile, "what could be the use of your asking God to let you go to heaven, when He is asking you Himself to come?"

May looked puzzled; for Ernest's words now seemed so different from his last.

"I thought you said I couldn't go, Master Ernest."

"Don't you know the gospel?" asked Ernest; "don't you know that God loves you, and wants to have you in heaven, though you are so bad; and that the Lord Jesus Christ died on the cross, that sinners might not die? Haven't you heard about His dying on the cross?"

"I've heard about the cross," said May, after thinking for a little. "Yes, I mind now; when first we came to the town I heard a blind man reading about it in the street. 'Twas dreadful; but I had to come away in the middle; and I didn't know it had anything to do with me."

"Oh, May," said Ernest, and a light of more than earthly beauty shone over his young face, for it was his heart's grateful answer that spoke in his eyes; "it was because God loved us that it all happened to His Son. It was because God so loved the world, that He let them treat His only begotten Son so. God loved you and me, and all of us, and He wanted us not to go down to that dreadful place, and so He punished His own dear Son instead. Think of how God must have loved us, and of how it must have made the Lord Jesus so frightfully unhappy for His Father to treat Him so. May, I love the Lord Jesus Christ with all my heart when I think of it; for He was the very best and kindest, and most loving and unselfish person in all the world; and it makes me ever so happy to think He loved me enough to die for me, and that He loves me now, and that I shall live with Him forever."

May gazed at Ernest; and as she saw the happy light glow in his face, and heard him tell the joy that made him so glad, it awoke a deep, deep wish in her heart.

"Oh, Master Ernest, do you think he'd love me that way too? Did you say it was me as well as you?"

"Listen to what God says, May. God loved you just the same. Don't you see, God loved everybody; and God made everybody, so He knows all about every one. And He says that whoever believes in His Son shall have everlasting life. Don't you know what everlasting life means? It means to go on living as happy as you can be forever."

These were strange things that May was hearing for the first time, and the glad tidings of great joy sounded very sweet in her ears. Could it be true? Could it be that the Son of the great God who lived in heaven cared about her, and loved her with a love of which she had never had an idea before? Her own father had loved her, she had thought; but she had found that his love could not be so very deep; and now as Ernest Vernon told her of God's great love, and of the joy that made his own heart so glad, and as she heard of the deep anguish of the sinless One who had died in torture because of the wicked things that she had done, the tears rose to her eyes and fell on the floor.

"What are you crying for, May?" asked Ernest gently. "Is it because you are sorry, or because you are glad? You ought to be ever so glad, you know, if you believe what God says."

But May did not answer, for her head was falling lower and lower, and the tears were gathering in her eyes, so that she could hardly see. Presently her head bowed on her hands, and a deep sob broke from her heart, as she said in a quivering voice –

"I daresay it's true for you, Master Ernest, but I don't see as how it ever could be for me."

"Well, but," said Ernest, "don't you see it is very wrong of you to say that. God says it is for whosoever believes in His Son. Don't you believe what God says, May?"

"Then I haven't got to ask at all," said May, after a long pause. "Why, Master Ernest, do you ever mean that all I've got to do is to be glad that God was so kind? I don't see as how there's anything else, if God really does say them things."

"God really does," said Ernest, in a sweet grave voice. "Haven't I just told you His own words? And indeed, May, that is all you have to do; because if you believe what God says, and take it for yourself, it must make you happy."

They had been talking for a long time; but they did not notice how quickly the time was slipping by, and May was entirely forgetful that there was a great deal of work undone downstairs that was waiting for her; but it was a time when the angels of God would watch to rejoice, and celebrate the birthday of another of God's children.

Ernest looked up, and May started, and the colour rushed to her face, while the returning consciousness of her household duties came back to her as she heard Ellen's astonished voice, "Well, I never! If I haven't been looking all over the house everywhere after you, and then to think of finding you here. There's missus half wild with business, and me too. What on earth are you about here, May?"

"Never mind," said Ernest; "I assure you, Ellen, May has been very well employed, so you must please not scold her, will you now?"

And Ernest spoke so gently, and there was such a sweet, kind smile on his face, that Ellen could not find it in her heart to be very angry.

"May," said Ernest, "just stop; I want to talk to you again. To-morrow is Sunday; do you think you could come up to-morrow afternoon, when the others are all out?

"I might. I'll try, Master Ernest, and thank you ever so much. But I must go now, please. Thank you, Master Ernest."

"What a queer girl you are, May," said Ellen, as she met her on the stairs, "to be talking that way to that young gentleman. He don't care about your father being gone; but I daresay he thought it was very good fun to hear you talk."

"It wasn't about that we was talking," said May in a low voice. But happily Ellen did not ask any more questions, as May was not willing to tell her about her talk with Ernest.

It was very late that Saturday night before May's work was done, and she lay on her hard little bed, near Ellen's. All the day while she had been running here and there, great thoughts had occupied her mind, and the serious look that shadowed her eyes was caused by the strange, sweet, new things of which Ernest had been speaking. Was it wonderful that she should think? Is it not far more wonderful that every one does not, and that men and women and children should go on living their life, which they know can only last for such a short time, all unheeding that life which is to last forever? God's great love offers His great gift of eternal life to whosoever will; and yet how many, how sadly many, there are who live without it, and who go away, away into the dim, lone eternity, without accepting the gift that might make them so glad. But it needs that the Holy Spirit of God should open men's eyes.

Might she really go to heaven? Could it really be true? Master Ernest had spoken about everlasting life, and that God would give it without being asked. "Oh," thought May, "if I could just hear Him say so Himself!" And then again she remembered that He had said so once; for might she not reckon as confidently on God's holy word as if she had heard His voice sounding from the deep blue above, and saying, "May Wood, you may come to heaven; everlasting life is yours."

And it made her very happy to take this into her heart, and to rest on the promise of the unchanging God.

But the next day, when the afternoon came, there was an anxious, weary look on May's face, and the sunny joy that the night time had veiled was a little clouded now.

Mrs. Bond had set out early in the morning for a day in the country; and when the dinners were over, and most of the people in the house had gone out, Ellen said –

"You can go out this afternoon, May, if you've a mind. I'll stop at home and take the evening. I think 'twould be better for you to go now."

"No, thank you," said May; "I haven't no-where to go; you can go now, and in the evening too, if you like."

"You're very accommodating," said Ellen; "but you'd better go somewhere, child. Why couldn't you go to the Park?"

"No, Ellen," said May earnestly; "please I'd really rather stay at home."

"Well, as you please." So if you really would rather stay, I think I might as well go. We neither of us get the chance too often, I should think."

This was just what May wished; for she was longing for the time when Ellen should go out, that she might talk again with Ernest Vernon.

Ernest had told his mother about his talk with their little servant girl, of how ignorant she was, and that she had seemed so glad to hear the joy-bringing message that they knew so well; and when the afternoon came, she had taken away the other children, and left him alone, so that if May should come, he might speak to her again.

By and by, as he was waiting there, a soft, slow footstep sounded, and then stopped; presently Ernest heard a hesitating little tap at the door, and when he quickly went and opened it, he found little May standing there, with a clean white apron on, and her curly hair brushed smoothly back.

"Oh, come in, May," said Ernest; "you need not be afraid; every one else has gone out, and my mother said you might come."

May came softly in, looking half pleased and half shy.

"Please, Master Ernest," she said, as Ernest made her sit down at the table, and fetched his mother's large Bible, "I've been thinking ever so much of what you was saying, and it did make me so glad that first night to think 'twas true."

"And doesn't it make you glad now?"

"Well, I don't know," May answered, the tears gathering in her eyes; "it do seem too good for me; and then –"

May stopped, and the tears fell on her white apron.

"Well, what then?" asked Ernest gently.

"Oh, Master Ernest, I've been ever so wicked, and specially since I've comed to the town; and it don't seem as if God would let me come to heaven, without I tried to be as good as good could be, to make up, and maybe not then. I've been a trying, but I keeps wicked; and I do get so tired."

"Poor May," said Ernest, "I wish you could see; and it is so very easy. Just listen."

Ernest laid his hands on the large Bible, and a grave seriousness settled on his face as he spoke.

"You see, May, it is quite right for you to see that you have been wicked, because you have. I daresay you may have been very wicked indeed, and nobody but God knows. And I think it is such a comfort that God does know, because He says, 'Through this Man' (that is, the Lord Jesus Christ) 'is preached unto you the forgiveness of sins.' Now isn't that very easy? You want the forgiveness of your sins, and God gives it to you, before you thought of wanting it. Well, I was going to say it is quite right that you should feel you ought to be punished for your wrong doings, because then it will make you so glad and thankful to the Lord Jesus for letting them punish Him instead of you. Can't you see that, May? Just think of these little words, 'Jesus was punished instead of me.'"

"But are you sure 'twas me, Master Ernest? Are you quite sure? Oh dear, dear, if it was!" May's face was intensely eager, and her voice trembled as she spoke.

"I'm more sure than of anything else in the whole wide world, because God says it. Surely you don't think God would say what was not true, May?" asked Ernest solemnly.

"Well, then, Master Ernest," said May, after a long time of waiting, and as she turned to him now a sunny joy seemed dancing in the tears that were still in her eyes, "I've got something to make me glad always. Am I really going to heaven? Am I sure to go? 'Cause I have comed to Him, and He knows everything, so He knows that. And I do believe what God says, 'cause God wouldn't tell a lie; that would be a dreadful bad thing to say, almost worse than the other bad things I've done."

"It would be the very worst thing of all," said Ernest.

They did not say anything more just for a little while. Very glad was little Ernest, and his heart was thanking God now, as he sat at the table near the large Bible. And May was glad; her heart was singing, for she was believing what God had said, and taking what God had given; and when any one does that, it must make them glad.

By and by May spoke again; but she was hardly speaking to Ernest, for she had almost forgotten that there was any one in the room, as she said very softly –

"I do so want to see Him. I would so like to."

"You will some day," said Ernest.

But soon there was a ring at the house door, and May knew that this was Ellen returning from her afternoon walk, and that she must open the door for her, and then help her to get the tea ready for the various lodgers in the different rooms.

So she rose to go; but as she stood at the door, she said timidly, "Master Ernest, I should like –"

"Well, what?" asked Ernest.

"I should like to shake hands with you, Master Ernest, if I might. 'Twas you told me, you know, about the Lord Jesus and eternal life."

"Indeed you may," said Ernest heartily, as he gave her his hand. "And May, you don't know how glad it has made me to think I have told you. You don't know how happy it makes me to think that I have made the Lord Jesus glad, and that He is looking at me and is pleased. And," said Ernest, as May was going, "I want you to remember this – what the Lord Jesus gives you. He gives you the forgiveness of sins, and eternal life; and He gave Himself for you; and He will love you and take care of you forever. Isn't that enough to make anybody happy?"

CHAPTER 5

ELLEN'S STORY

It was several weeks now since Thomas Wood had left his little girl alone in the great city. She had not heard anything about him since then. May did not think about getting a letter by the post; for she had never had such a thing in her life, and she could not have read it if she had.

Sometimes she thought a great deal about her father, wondering what he was doing, where he was, and when she should see him again. Sometimes, in the middle of her daily work, Ellen's brisk voice would arouse her from a dreamy reverie. The tears would come into her blue eyes now and then, as she thought of her distant home on the hills, and of the days that she had passed there; she remembered the cool, quiet cottage, with its blossoming garment, where the white flowers starred the green; and when her hot, dusty toil made her weary now, it seemed all the sweeter. Then, when the evening drew its shady curtain over the city, and the lamps shone away the soft twilight hours, while the noise of traffic and labour rose as loud as ever, her thoughts would fly wistfully back to the cottage-door, where she had sat on just such summer evenings, waiting to see her father climb up the grassy hill. May hardly knew what waiting meant now-a-days; for every moment of the day seemed to be filled up in one way or another.

But then when these thoughts came into her mind, she would put them away by looking onward, and thinking of the great joy that God had given her, and of the bright, happy home, where she would live forever with the kind Lord Jesus, who had loved her so much as to die for her. "The Lord Jesus loves me a deal better than father ever did," said May to herself; "and oh, but I do love Him, and it will be so happy to be in heaven with Him!"

Now she knew that God would let her come to heaven; that He had given His gracious invitation long before she had thought of wanting it, and that it was the joy of the Lord Jesus to have her there with Him, that she might behold His glory. Her little desolate heart had found its home now; for it was given to the One who, the better He is known, the more He will be found worthy of love and trust.

Before Ernest Vernon had left Mrs. Bond's lodgings, he and May had had several sweet talks together, and Ernest had read to May many chapters from the blessed book that God has given; and as she listened to the words that tell of when her loving Saviour "went about doing good," working such gracious works of power, and saying such kind words, her heart answered with a deep adoring love, and thrilled with a trusting joy, to think that the powerful, wise, and kind God-man was her Master, and her loving Saviour, the One who knew all about her, and had promised to take care of her forever.

For Ernest Vernon had gone away now, and May missed her young teacher sadly. The father had arrived the evening before they had left, and May had been the one to open the door for him, and to usher him into the drawing-room. It gave her a little heart-ache as she saw the children's glad welcome to him, and the loving, kind way in which he had greeted them all; and when in the evening she had to come into the room, she saw the father again, with the children all clustered around him, and little Nellie, the youngest, seated on his knee, it seemed to May as if the Vernons ought to be happy wherever they went, for they were all going together.

They had gone away now, and the ship was bearing them very far from the busy city, over the restless, white-crested ocean waves, to the sunny country where they were going to live.

One morning, not very long after the Vernons had left the house, and new lodgers were occupying their rooms, May had answered the postman's knock, and, as usual, she carried the letters to Mrs. Bond, who looked at the addresses, and then held one towards May, who could not quite understand what she meant.

"Take it, child," said Mrs. Bond, as she still held it towards her.

"Where to, please ma'am?" asked May.

"Where to? Why, wherever you like."

But still May did not understand that the letter was for her.

"Don't you see it's for you? Your name's May Wood, isn't it? And I'm glad to see that your friends address your letters in a sensible way."

"A letter for me!" May was surprised, and very much delighted too. It could only be from her father, of course; and if he could have seen the dancing joy in his little girl's eyes, it would have repaid Thomas Wood for the trouble it gave him to write that letter.

"O Ellen, Ellen!" said May, as she mounted the stairs more quickly than she was accustomed, and ran against her fellow-servant at the top of the first flight; "whatever do you think? Father's been and writ to me! I've got the letter! Well, if I'd known it was coming when I got up this morning, how different I should have felt."

"What's the good of a letter, if you can't read it?" asked Ellen, smiling.

"Ah, but you're such a dear old thing; you'll do that, I know. Here, Ellen, do read it now. Would there be time?"

"Oh, there's time, if I choose," said Ellen.

Thomas Wood's letter was not a very happy or hopeful one. It spoke of a great many things that did not please him, and of very little that did; he spoke of the hardness of the times and of the badness of wages; and then he said, "I sometimes wish we was back home. It might have been as well if we had let well alone. Maybe we might some day."

"Tell you what, May," said Ellen, as she finished reading the letter, "I think your father's a rolling-stone, and they say rolling-stones don't gather no moss."

"He's my father, you see," said May gravely.

"Wonder where my father is?" said Ellen presently.

"Don't you know?" asked May, surprised.

"No, nor care," said Ellen. Then as if she wished to change the subject, she said –

"May, you must get on with your reading. Look here, you must know how, you know. So we'll do this: we'll get up a quarter of an hour earlier every morning and try at it, and then I think you'll get on."

"I do want to know how to read," said May; "and I have a reason for wanting to know now more than every I had before."

"What is it?" asked Ellen.

"Well," said May, hesitating, for she knew Ellen would not like her to say it, "I want to read the Bible every day."

"What in the world do you want to do that for?" asked Ellen. "I do believe you're getting religious, May."

"I don't think I am," said May. "What is religious?"

"What is it? Just as if you didn't know. But I'll tell you what I think being religious is, if you like; it's thinking yourself ever so much better than any one else, and looking as miserable as you can always."

"Well, I'm not religious then," said May; "for I'm sure I ain't better than any one else; and I don't think I look particular miserable, do I? But I expect you mean being a Christian; and I am that, Ellen."

"You are!" said Ellen. "And what am I, then? – a heathen, I suppose!"

May looked very earnestly indeed at Ellen, and there was a wistful gaze of loving entreaty in her eyes, as they met Ellen's, that showed how her heart was feeling. For May had been thinking a great deal about what Ellen was, and what she was not. She loved her fellow-servant, who had been so kind to her when no one else had been there to speak to her desolate little heart; and often in these few weeks, since she had begun to rejoice in her own glad portion, she had wished and prayed that Ellen might do the same; for May really believed what God had said. And those hours when Ernest had read to her God's message of love had been spent to good purpose; she had a good natural memory; and many of the texts that he had read several times to her she remembered now. She remembered what God had said about the everlasting portion of bitterness and woe that awaits those who refuse His kindness and grace; and then, as the names of her father and Ellen, and of others that she knew, came into her mind, it made her anxious heart ache to think of them; for she could not but fear that they did not know and love the Saviour who was so dear to her. May was not "judging" them; oh, no! for how gladly would she have said that they did, and that they also were going to that bright land, where all is rest and gladness. It seemed a wonderful thing to May, that people should know anything about all this joy and treasure and not heed it.

So that it was very anxiously, and with the soft tears in her earnest eyes, that May drew a little closer to Ellen, and said, "Oh, Ellen! What are you? I wish you was a Christian!"

"Well," said Ellen, "you may just as well give up wishing that for me then. I'm not one, and I never shall be."

"Why, Ellen," said May, "you can have nothing happy to think about at all then, hardly; because, you know, there's not much use thinking about nice things that's going to happen here, 'cause maybe they won't happen at all; and if they does, they're so soon over."

"You just mind your own business," said Ellen gruffly.

Just then Mrs. Bond's bell downstairs was heard violently ringing, which showed that she was not pleased by the absence of both her servants. Ellen gave herself an impatient jerk. "I never seen such a woman for bells," she said. "Oh, then indeed you're about right, there's not very much to make me care about anything."

May had only just time to put her hand on Ellen's shoulder, and look tenderly in her face. "Oh, Ellen," she said, "I do wish you was a Christian! Never mind the things that make you happy here; the Lord Jesus can do it so much better, and it is so nice to be thinking about Him and about heaven."

"The things that make me happy!" said Ellen, with a very hard, bitter laugh, and a look of such aching woe, that it went to May's heart. "I tell you, child, I haven't nothing to make me happy, and never, never shall."

Poor Ellen! She was unhappy indeed. Her life was a shaded one; for its morning brightness had been overclouded by sorrow and disappointment. The sun had passed away, and no hope of "dawning bright" to come made her glad; for the cruel enemy of joy and rest had hung the veil of unbelief before her. Her heart could wail a bitter echo to the words –

> "All that my soul has tried
> Left but a dismal void."

But she had learnt no soul melody for the rest.

> "Jesus has satisfied;
> Jesus is mine."

And so she was moody, and sullen, and passionate; bitter against those around her, and

"Oh, Ellen," she said, "I do wish you was a Christian."—
Page 72.

speaking in harsh words, which she did not really feel, of those who said that they were Christians.

But she told something of her heart's bitter sorrow and unrest to little May that evening.

That day Ellen was more sullen and opposing than usual with her mistress; and although Mrs. Bond's easy-going nature bore more than perhaps some people would have done, for the sake of quiet, she was really provoked at last, and she told Ellen that if she behaved in that way she had better find some other situation; at which Ellen became more angry, and said that she would, and that she would not stay another week, no, nor another night, in her house.

Both Mrs. Bond and her servant were very angry, as Ellen flung herself out of the room, upstairs into the little garret chamber that had witnessed May's trouble so often. But when Ellen had been there for a little while, she changed her mind about the threat of going away that night, and she knew that Mrs. Bond would not force her to fulfil her angry promise; for it would not be at all convenient for her that one of her servants should suddenly go away.

When May came up late that night, she found that the door was locked. She knocked once or twice; but as no answer came, she said –

"Please, Ellen, won't you open the door?"

A hasty movement inside, and then the lock was sharply turned; and as May came in, Ellen turned quickly away to take her place by the open window, where she had been before. May could not see her face; but something in Ellen's attitude as she sat there showed her that the storm of ill feeling had not yet passed away, and there was not a word said on either side for some minutes.

At length May broke the silence by saying, "Missus was real angry."

"Angry!" said Ellen. "And I was angry too, I can tell you. And would you like to know whose fault it was that I went on as I did?"

"Well," said May gently, "I thought it was your own fault, Ellen."

"Then it was yours," said Ellen. "So there!"

"Mine, Ellen? My fault?" asked May, astonished.

But Ellen seemed not to intend to say any more just then. Poor May was perplexed as well as sorry; she did not understand what Ellen meant, and she did not see how her strange, passionate ways could be her fault. It was rather unkind, she thought; for she did not understand the gloomy bitterness in Ellen's heart that found vent in these hard ways and words.

"La, child! Whatever have you got to cry about?" asked Ellen. "I didn't mean you'd done anything bad."

"Ellen," said May, as a thought of Ellen's feelings came across her mind, "what did you mean?"

"I'll tell you what I meant," said Ellen, almost fiercely, as she turned sharply round and faced May

– "I meant that it was you talking like you did this morning. It was you saying about how happy you was, and about how there's nothing down here to make any one happy. It was you making me think of what I won't think about. Why should you be happy, and not me? Never me, – never, never."

These last words Ellen almost gasped, as she rose from her chair and walked quickly to the other side of the room and back again. Then she sat down by the bedside, and buried her face in her hands.

May came and put her arms around her, and said in a soft, trembling voice, for she was a little frightened at Ellen's vehemence, "Darling Ellen, Ellen dear, I'm afraid you're so miserable."

There came a sigh that seemed to echo in the hopelessness of her heart's hollow depth – "God knows I am."

"And God cares," whispered May.

"May," said Ellen, "you must not speak to me like that. I can't bear it. Oh, May, May!" sobbed Ellen.

May was frightened. She had strong feelings herself; but she knew nothing of the pent-up storm and torrent of passionate feelings that she saw now, as Ellen suddenly threw out her arms and pressed them around her. It seemed as if the intensity of her feelings was expressed in that grasp.

"I tried to be a Christian once, I did! And I thought I was one for a bit; but I wasn't. Oh, dear, dear!"

And now the flood of gasping sobs began, deep, tearless sobs, that seemed breaking from her very heart. And the tears came, such a flood of bitter weeping, as Ellen swayed herself backwards and forwards, moaning and striking her head against the bedside, in a weary, despairing way, as she clutched at the bed-clothes or anything near, as if seeking for something – anything to grasp and help her.

By and by she stopped the sobbing and swaying to and fro, and leaned heavily against May, half crouching and half lying on the floor.

"I'm hungry, hungry, and I've got nothing!" she moaned in a broken voice.

May felt, though she did not know the words, "He satisfieth the hungry with good things."

After a little time Ellen raised her head, and looked sadly and wearily at May; then she shook the clinging black hair from her pale, sorrowful face, and said, "What is being a Christian?"

"Isn't it believing what God says?" asked May.

"It's more than that, I know," said Ellen. "It's being good. It's giving up doing things that you liked to do before. It's repenting," she said, with bitter emphasis.

"Well," said May, after a little time for thinking, "if you really love the Lord Jesus very much, I think you'll be able to do things that He likes; because, you know, He loves you so, and He is so very kind."

"I believe you do," said Ellen with the faintest shadow of a smile, "because I've watched you."

It was a glad summer smile that broke over May's face as she said, "I do try." But then it became graver as she remembered the dreary aching in Ellen's heart, and she said, "I don't think I know what repenting means."

"It means being very sorry that you've been wicked. And I ain't sorry; I'm only frightened. I don't think I should care at all, only that I know God punishes people for being wicked."

You see, May had not learnt very much yet, so she could not explain to Ellen that repentance means changing one's mind, and turning to God.

The jailer at Philippi repented when he believed on the Lord Jesus Christ; and every poor sinner who comes with all his vileness and wrong feelings, labouring and heavy-laden, to the Saviour's feet, is in reality repenting; for he has turned from the way of everlasting destruction, and he has turned to God. And when God shows this poor sinner how He has loved him in spite of his wickedness, and what He has done for him, will it not melt his heart? Will it not make him try to avoid the things that the loving God hates, and try to do something to please Him?

"May," said Ellen, after another silence, "I tried to be good once. I thought I was nearly a Christian once, when I was ill. But I soon found out I weren't. I'll tell you. Long ago, oh, ever so long ago!" she said, with a deep, weary sigh, and a look in her eyes that seemed to see back into a time and place far distant from the present one, and yet it was not very long ago, "I was a wild young thing, just about as old as you be now; and I lived at home, with my sister and my brother Harry. Father lived at home too, and he used to go on bad; but I didn't heed that much then. Jessie used to fret about him night and day, I believe; but I didn't mind, for Harry always brought home his wages; and we had enough.

"We lived near the sea. You never seen the sea, so you can't tell what it's like; and I don't think I could make you know. You couldn't without you saw it. Harry was partners in a fishing-boat, and he used to go out for days together. Sometimes he'd be off early, ever so early, in the morning, and I'd get up and go with him to the boat. We used to walk along together, we two, over the common till we got to the top of the cliffs. And then we'd be near the sea, and feel the wind come blowing in fit to blow you down. You never feel that way here in the town; it's a kind of feeling that made you want to run, and made you feel so glad that the wind was blowing, and that the waves was dashing down below on the rocks, and that the sun was making the sea look glad.

"And Harry used to take hold of my hand; and then we'd run until we was out of breath, and getting down close to the water, so that when I'd call out to Harry that I could go no further, the roaring and the dashing that the waves made was so loud that I could scarcely hear myself.

"I was happy then and I thought everything was going to be like that always, only better. I seemed to feel that what was coming must be nice. And I used to think about it all, and Jessie and I used to talk about it; that is, I used to tell her about all the things that I was going to do, and how we'd get on, and Harry would make it all so happy. I don't know which of the two I loved best; for I couldn't have loved either more than I did.

"But sometimes, when I'd talk to Jessie about what we'd do, she'd only smile and say nothing; only sometimes she'd say she thought she wouldn't live very long; she thought she was going to heaven; and she used to talk like you do now, and ask me not to fret when she was gone. I didn't believe her until I had to; for at last I saw she was dying; but I didn't quite believe it until I saw her lying so white and cold, and nothing, nothing could move her.

"And she was buried in a place where you can hear the waves and the wind. I can see the place now, and I can feel the wind come blowing in, and hear the noise it makes, like some one angry and crying. But I can't see the place where Harry's lying, for he's underneath the waves. Oh, didn't I wish I was too! Didn't I wish, after they'd brought me home, thinking I was drowned too, that I was really, and that I had stayed under the waves when I went down with Harry.

"I never can tell how it was exactly, and I don't think I want to know. Only it was one morning, after we'd walked down to the boat, and after we'd been looking at the sun making the white of the waves look yellow-like, and the sea-gulls' wings had a silvery look; and then Harry said if I'd come he'd take me out a little way, 'cause he had the boat to himself that day. So we went a long way out; for we got talking, and I was so lonesome all day by myself at home, that I did not want to go back.

"I don't know how it was; I never can tell. I know the sky got black all on a sudden, and the waves was as big as green mountains; and when I caught hold of Harry, as frightened as could be, he laughed, and said there was no danger. But there was, and I don't know how it happened that Harry went down, and never came up no more, and that another boat found me. I know I wished they'd left me where I was. Oh, Harry, Harry, and little Jessie! I wish I could see you just once again.

"Then I was ill, very ill, so that they thought I should die; and even a long time after that they thought I should go off into a decline. A lady used to come and talk to me sometimes, and I thought I was getting to be a Christian. I used to feel so, lying there; and I thought when I got well I'd be so different.

"But I wasn't. The very first day I got up I got into a passion with another girl; and as I got better I began to feel all the bad feelings just the same; and I went on with father like mad, until he told me he didn't want me to stop at home any more; so I heard of a place in the town, and I came here.

"That showed me I was no Christian. And oh! I tried hard to be one afore I gave it up. But I couldn't repent, and there was no good trying to make myself think I did. Besides, I didn't feel like a Christian; I didn't feel a bit happy, nor as if my sins were forgiven. I used to feel half mad sometimes, going round and round, and over and over, trying if I couldn't feel right. I mind when I used to hear people singing –

'How sweet the name of Jesus sounds.'

It used to make me cry; oh dear! How I cried, so that I thought I couldn't cry again, until you made me to-night; for I knew the name of Jesus didn't sound sweet to me; it made me frightened; only I knew if I was a Christian, how sweet it would sound to me. Oh, May, May!" said Ellen, with a groan of deep heart anguish, "if I could only say I was a Christian! If I could only feel my sins was forgiven!"

"Ellen," said little May, with the tears running down her own cheeks, and her arms thrown around Ellen's crouching figure, "I do wish you was. I don't know how it is, but I don't think much about the feeling. I know my sins is forgiven, 'cause God says so."

"God don't say it about me," said Ellen sadly.

"But He does, Ellen, if you believe on the Lord Jesus Christ."

"Well, I suppose I don't then."

"Why don't you then?" asked May. "Why don't you now? You can, you know, this very minute. Maybe you do. And yet you ought to be happy if you do. You know, Ellen, if you believe on Him, your sins is forgiven whether you feel they are or not. I wonder," said May half to herself, "could any one believe and be a Christian without knowing it?"

Ellen soon fell back into deep silence, and her silence was not easily broken by any one but herself. So they did not speak again as they had spoken that night, until just before she went away.

For she did go away, in a month from that night. A restless spirit came over her, the restlessness of a heart that had not found its home, and which does not know a peace that the world cannot give.

The evening before she went away she turned suddenly to May, and said,

"May, now mind I don't want to talk. But promise me, will you pray for me?"

"I will, Ellen dear; I do already," said May earnestly. "And oh," she said, with her arms around her, "I wish you wasn't going. What shall I do when you're gone?"

"Oh, you'll get on much better, I daresay. And it don't much matter where I am."

Ellen went away; and she found another home amongst strangers.

Are you surprised to hear that Ellen became happy one day?

At last she stopped thinking about her own feelings, or about herself at all, and looking to the Saviour of the world as her Saviour, trusting in Him like a little child, she believed the glad, sweet things that God says about those who, ever so weakly, put their trust in His only begotten Son.

Are there not many who, saying from their hearts, "Other refuge have I none," yet go mourning and weary-hearted, because they think so much about themselves, and so little about Him who wishes them to be glad? And so they have little joy in their hearts, and little strength to please the Lord, and to be able to resist the flood of evil against them.

And now May felt as if another friend was gone; which, indeed, was true; for the servant who came to fill Ellen's place had none of her kind feelings towards the younger girl, and a great deal more labour and care fell to May's share, without Ellen's sympathy to lighten them.

She had been ailing for some little time, but tried to do her best; and as the little servant girl thought of the Eye of Love looking down from heaven and seeing her, it made her happy to think that she was pleasing her Master, for her heart had answered to His voice – "Follow thou Me."

But she was very tired; her strength was not equal to the labour required of her, and often when the night time came, it was a very pale, exhausted little form that lay on the bed in the garret chamber.

And Mrs. Bond did not notice that the colour was fading from the cheeks of the country girl, and that the light in her eye was becoming dim; it was not her way to notice such things unless she was obliged.

One day as May was passing quickly along the street, where her mistress's errands had brought her, her quick eye fancied that the figure of a man, walking at some little distance from her, was not unknown to her. It took her back to the old times in Farleigh village, when she had watched in the evening for her father's coming home. For it was he; and her heart gave a glad bound to meet him. It was so long since she had seen him, or since she had heard anything about him; it seemed so very long since any one had spoken to her a word of loving care, and there was a glad little tumult of joy in her heart as she hurried to meet him.

But, to her surprise, he was passing her at first, and she had given a little cry of joy before he stopped, and then she said –

"Why, Father, is it you? Don't you see me? It's me, Father; it's May."

"May, child," he said, "is that ever you? Why, what's got to you, my darling? You're as white as you can be, and so thin."

And May forgot the busy street and the passers-by; she did not think of Mrs. Bond and the house-work; it was so sweet to see her father once more; it was such a glad, strange feeling to find that any one should care so much to see her, and she burst into a flood of tears; for she was weak and excited. "I be so glad, Father," she said presently. "I'm crying 'cause I'm so very glad, and it's so nice for anybody to call me darling."

Thomas Wood was reproaching himself in his heart. He saw the difference that there was in his child from the time when she had left her own country home, as fresh as one of the roses that adorned it, and a quick pang of fear came to his heart lest he should have found it out too late, and that his child should be going away, as her mother had gone.

For he had come to see her with an intention and a plan. He had quarreled with the men who had been his companions, and now he had come to the conclusion that, after all, the best thing for a man to do was to live with his own child, especially when she was such a sensible little maiden as he knew his to be.

The town where he was now living was not such a large or populous one as May's city home; there were many parts, not far from the streets and the trade, where the flowers grew and the fields spread their sloping green, and where the birds sang as sweetly as in their country nests near the Half-way hill. And it was his design that May and himself should find another cottage home in some such quiet place; "and then maybe the child will be satisfied," he said to himself; for he knew that there was not much to make her contented and happy in Mrs. Bond's house. So presently he spoke –

"May, would you like to come and live with father, again?"

"Oh, Father," said May, looking almost beseechingly in his face, "do you mean it? Don't say so if you don't."

And her trembling lips showed what an earnestness of feeling she had on the subject.

"Why shouldn't I mean it, child?" he asked. "'Twas foolish of me to think of living with them others. They're a bad set; and you and I won't quarrel, will we, my dear? But, May, whatever has come to you? Have you been ill?"

"Not quite bright, Father," said May with a sunny smile; "but I'll be all right now, I expect."

Mrs. Bond was not at all pleased when she found that May was going to leave her. She had found out the value of a servant who knows that she has a Master in heaven, who is always looking at her, and whose name is Love.

Little May became better. The change from her life of toil, and weariness, and late hours, and early rising, to the quiet cottage, which they found afterwards, went far toward strengthening her weary body, and making the country roses bloom on her cheeks again. It was so pleasant to rest, and to know that she might do so; and her eyes were glad to see other sights than those that always met them, where the houses clustered so thickly, and seemed almost to darken the sky's brightness overhead.

And May's heart's wish was that her dear father might know the joy that had made her so glad, when her earthly path had been a sorrowful one.

There were other people who lived near her new home who noticed her kind, loving words and ways; and they saw that there was a difference between her and the other girls around her.

So wandering May was a light in her quiet home; for she loved to speak of the One who had loved her with an everlasting love, and who had promised to make her glad forever.

———————

I heard the voice of Jesus say,
"Come unto Me, and rest;
Lay down, thou weary one, lay down
Thy head upon my breast!"
I came to Jesus as I was,
Weary, and worn, and sad;
I found in Him a resting place,
And He has made me glad.

I heard the voice of Jesus say,
"Behold, I freely give
The living water; thirsty one,
Stoop down, and drink, and live!"
I came to Jesus, and I drank
Of that life-giving stream;
My thirst was quenched, my soul revived,
And now I live in Him.

I heard the voice of Jesus say,
"I am this dark world's light;
Look unto Me; thy morn shall rise,
And all thy day be bright."
I looked to Jesus, and I found
In Him my Star, my Sun;
And in that light of life I'll walk
Till traveling days are done.